CONTENTS

CUBIX™

ROBOTS FOR EVERYONE

Pedigree®

Published by Pedigree Books Limited
The Old Rectory, Matford Lane, Exeter, EX2 4PS.
E-mail books@pedigreegroup.co.uk
Published 2002

£5.99

WHO'S WHO IN BUBBLE TOWN

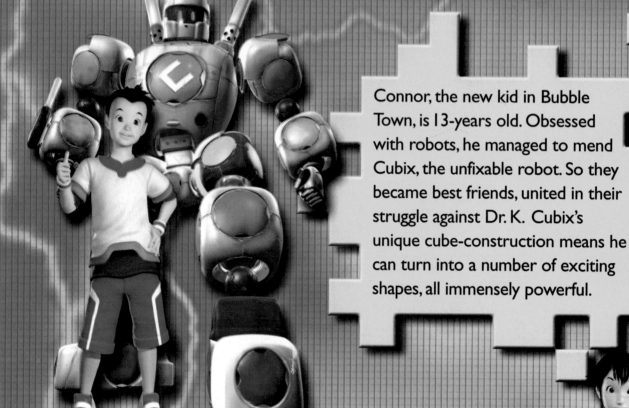

Connor, the new kid in Bubble Town, is 13-years old. Obsessed with robots, he managed to mend Cubix, the unfixable robot. So they became best friends, united in their struggle against Dr. K. Cubix's unique cube-construction means he can turn into a number of exciting shapes, all immensely powerful.

Hela is Bubble Town's robot expert. With the help of Diagnostix, whose head can separate from his body and fly on its own, she works at the Botties Pit, the town's finest robot repair centre. And she lets the kids hangout there provided they help to clean up and learn her robot-fixing skills.

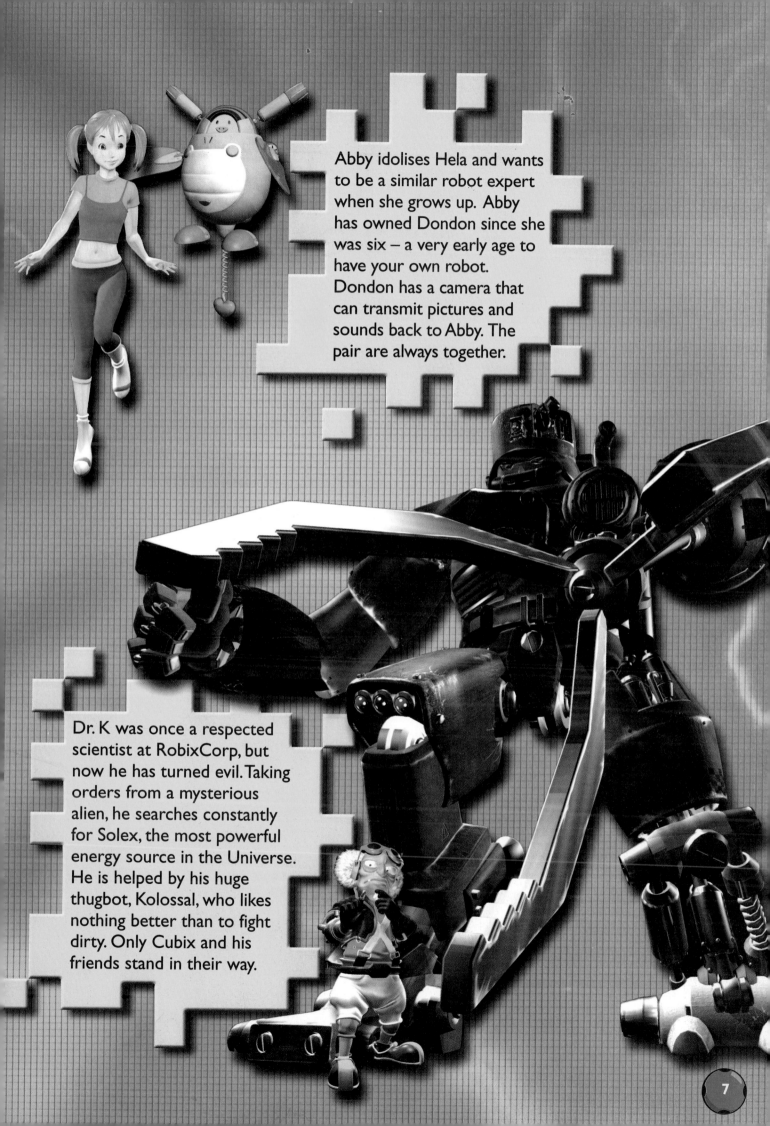

Abby idolises Hela and wants to be a similar robot expert when she grows up. Abby has owned Dondon since she was six – a very early age to have your own robot. Dondon has a camera that can transmit pictures and sounds back to Abby. The pair are always together.

Dr. K was once a respected scientist at RobixCorp, but now he has turned evil. Taking orders from a mysterious alien, he searches constantly for Solex, the most powerful energy source in the Universe. He is helped by his huge thugbot, Kolossal, who likes nothing better than to fight dirty. Only Cubix and his friends stand in their way.

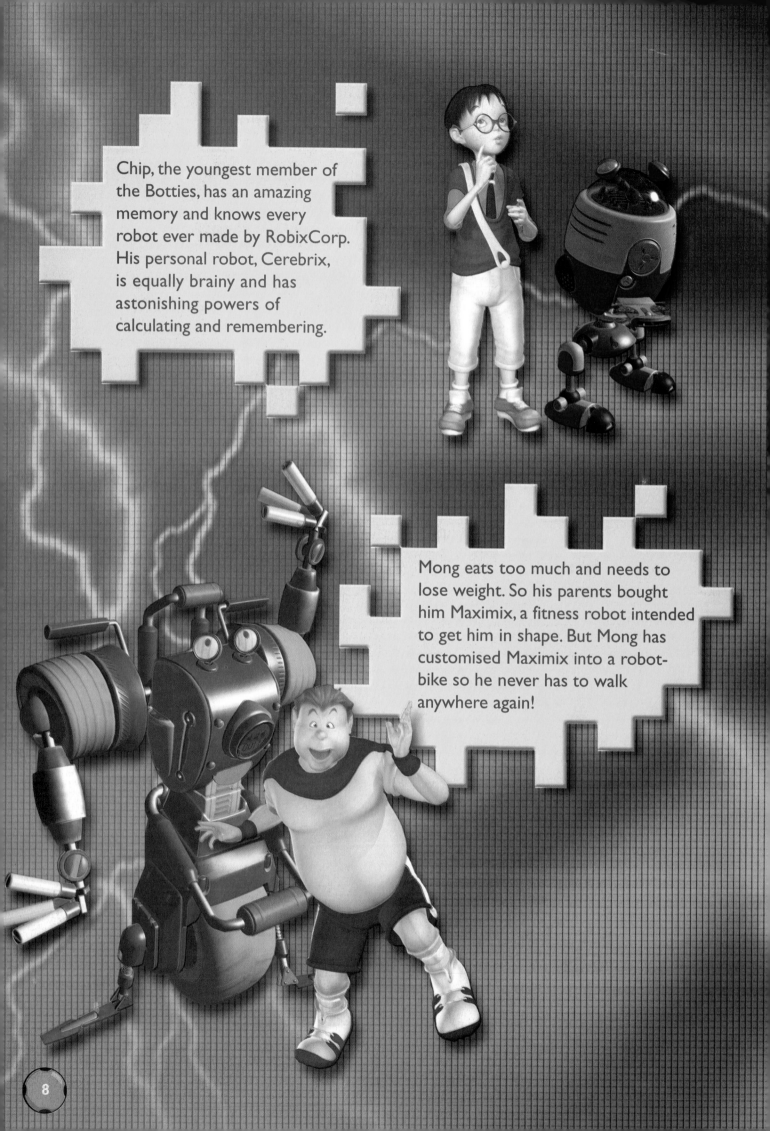

Chip, the youngest member of the Botties, has an amazing memory and knows every robot ever made by RobixCorp. His personal robot, Cerebrix, is equally brainy and has astonishing powers of calculating and remembering.

Mong eats too much and needs to lose weight. So his parents bought him Maximix, a fitness robot intended to get him in shape. But Mong has customised Maximix into a robot-bike so he never has to walk anywhere again!

AND NOT FORGETTING...

HOP2X™ Jumping taxi and personal transporter

LECTRX™ Lectrix, roams Bubble Town giving electric charges to robots that are short of power

MXMUTT™ Originally made as a pig, but given a dog's circuitry

DISPOSX™ Robot garbage disposal unit

Mr. FXIT™ Robotic robot fixer!

WELDNFX™ All-purpose construction worker

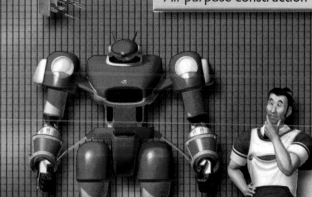

Graham, Connor's dad, runs the Doughnut Shop. HATES robots!!!

QUXTREME 5000™ Test-market robot

9

CEREBRIX™ **says**

SPOT THE DIFFERENCE

Chip's special robot is noted for his brainpower. He's ace at working things out. But are you?

To test your powers of observation, Cerebrix has set this puzzle. Can you spot six small differences between these two pictures of Cubix battling the mighty Kolossal?

THE UNFIXABLE ROBOT

Connor and his dad, Graham, were speeding along the highway in their hovercar. Connor looked excitedly out of the window at all the different robots passing by.

"Guess we'll be seeing lots of robots were we're goin'," chuckled Graham, unable to keep his secret any longer. "I bought us a house in that place you're always goin' on about."

"Bubble Town!" exclaimed Connor, who loved robots. "They have as many robots as people. Excellent!"

"Oh, sure. Excellent!" sighed Graham, who *hated* robots!

Later, in a quiet suburb of Bubble Town, Abby and her pet robot Dondon watched the newcomers arrive. They were so interested that they ignored a newsflash on TV, reporting a Botanix landscaping robot going out of control.

"Dondon, ready for a mission?" asked Abby. "Fly over and find out what you can!"

Dondon could send back sound and pictures to Abby. But he did not get much of a chance! Graham spotted him snooping outside their new house. He chased the little robot away and made him crash!

"Why won't you move, Dondon?" cried Abby, running over anxiously.

Connor fetched some tools and started work on the lifeless robot.

"Don't worry. I can fix him," he said.

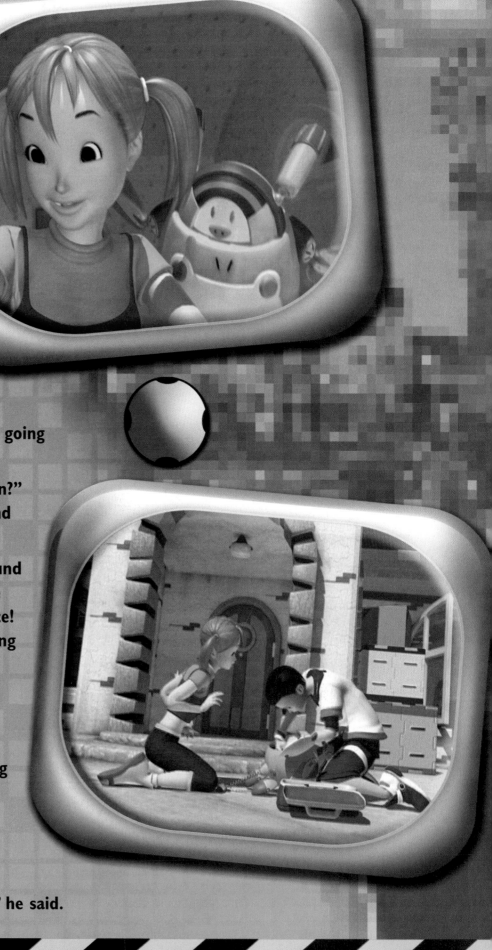

Connor brought Dondon back to life, but the robot's voice was still malfunctioning. So Abby decided to take him to the Botties Pit.

"It's the best robot repair shop in Bubble Town," explained Abby, as they sped through town on her hover scooter.

The Botties Pit was run by Hela who knew everything there is to know about robots.

Abby's friends, Mong and Chip, were there too. Hela let them hang out at her workshop provided they worked hard and learned about robots.

"It's really quite good," murmured Hela, checking the repair job that Connor had done to Dondon. "I must say, I'm impressed."

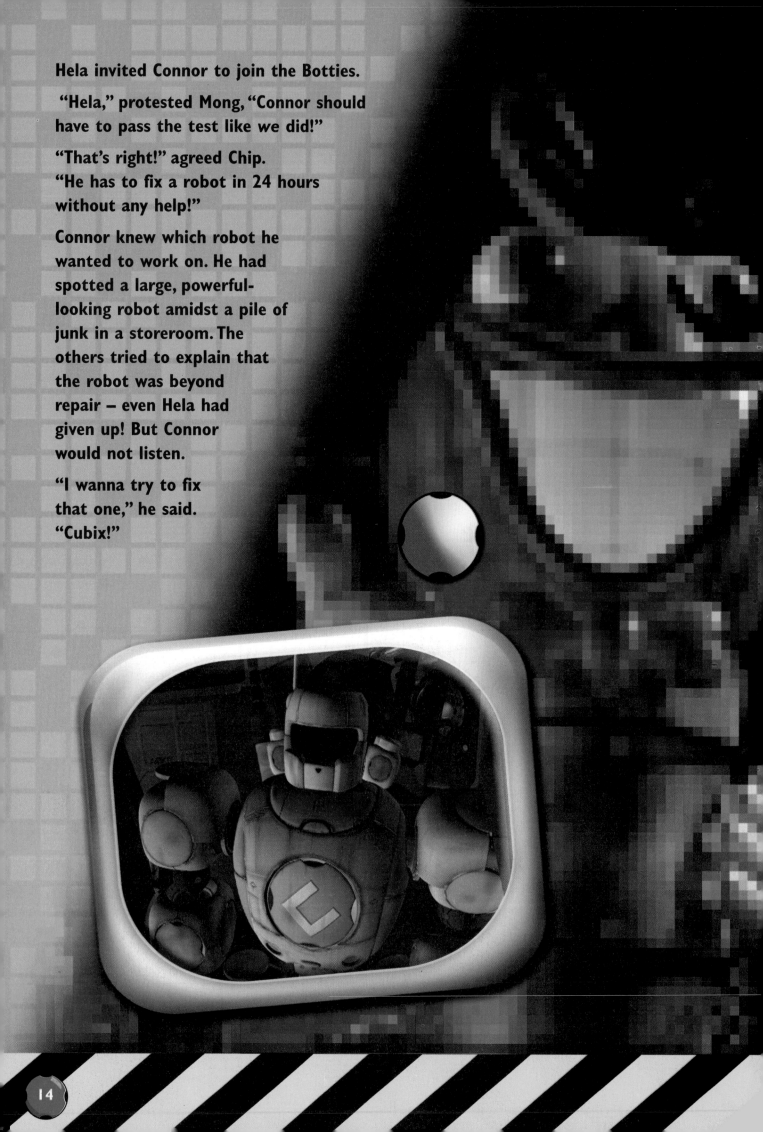

Hela invited Connor to join the Botties.

"Hela," protested Mong, "Connor should have to pass the test like we did!"

"That's right!" agreed Chip. "He has to fix a robot in 24 hours without any help!"

Connor knew which robot he wanted to work on. He had spotted a large, powerful-looking robot amidst a pile of junk in a storeroom. The others tried to explain that the robot was beyond repair – even Hela had given up! But Connor would not listen.

"I wanna try to fix that one," he said. "Cubix!"

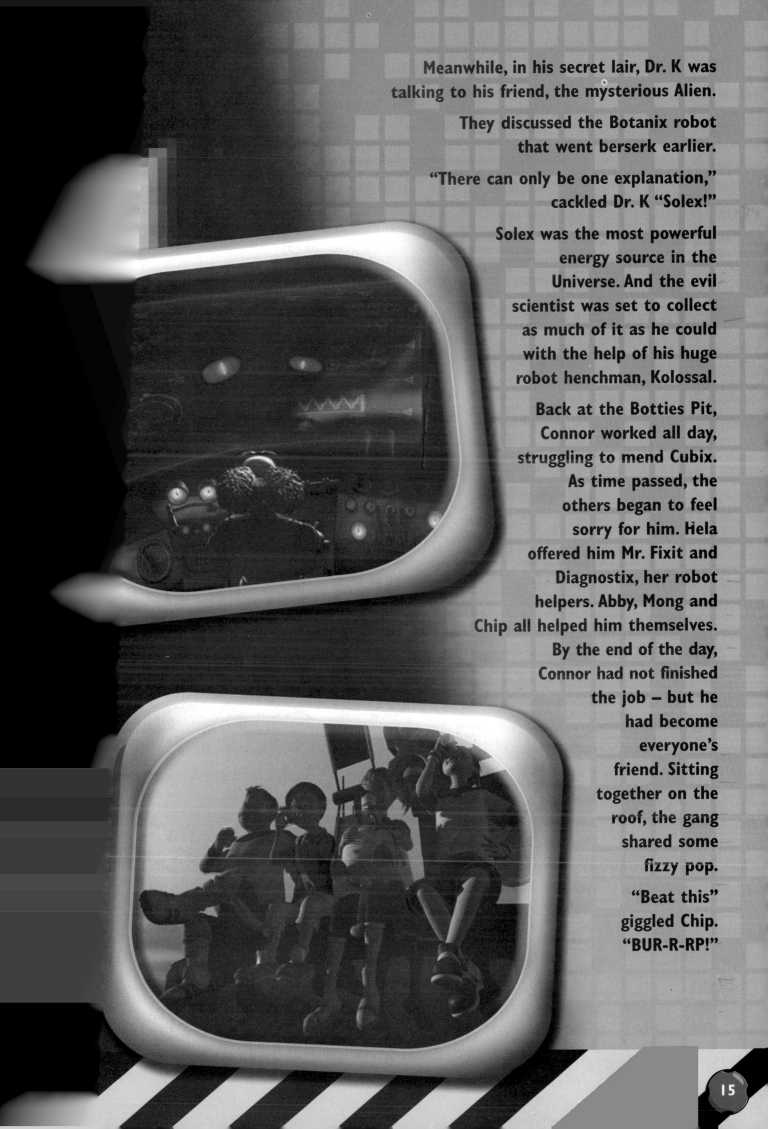

Meanwhile, in his secret lair, Dr. K was talking to his friend, the mysterious Alien.

They discussed the Botanix robot that went berserk earlier.

"There can only be one explanation," cackled Dr. K "Solex!"

Solex was the most powerful energy source in the Universe. And the evil scientist was set to collect as much of it as he could with the help of his huge robot henchman, Kolossal.

Back at the Botties Pit, Connor worked all day, struggling to mend Cubix. As time passed, the others began to feel sorry for him. Hela offered him Mr. Fixit and Diagnostix, her robot helpers. Abby, Mong and Chip all helped him themselves. By the end of the day, Connor had not finished the job – but he had become everyone's friend. Sitting together on the roof, the gang shared some fizzy pop.

"Beat this" giggled Chip. "BUR-R-RP!"

Despite toiling through the night until he was exhausted, Connor failed to get Cubix working. So he ran out of time and failed his test. Feeling like a complete failure, Connor walked sadly away.

"So long, Cubix," he sighed. "You would've made a great friend."

Little did he know that his words were igniting sparks of life deep within the silent robot!

Shortly afterwards, Hela arrived with another robot that had gone out of control. She was just starting to check the WeldNFix when Dr. K arrived outside with Kolossal.

His special detector-gun had told them that some Solex inside the robot had caused the malfunction and was up for grabs!

CRASH! Kolossal's extending metal arm smashed through the wall of the Botties Pit and snatched the WeldNFix.

"Excellent work," laughed Dr. K "Now, Kolossal, reel it in and let's get going!"

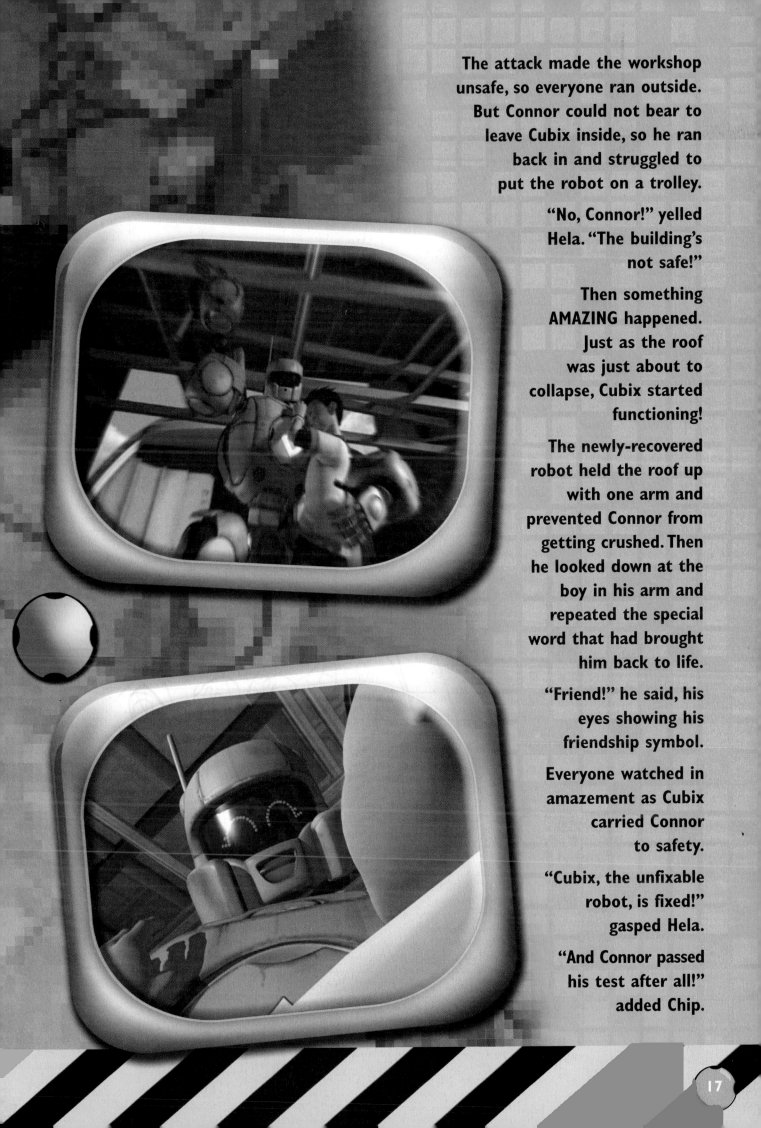

The attack made the workshop unsafe, so everyone ran outside. But Connor could not bear to leave Cubix inside, so he ran back in and struggled to put the robot on a trolley.

"No, Connor!" yelled Hela. "The building's not safe!"

Then something AMAZING happened. Just as the roof was just about to collapse, Cubix started functioning!

The newly-recovered robot held the roof up with one arm and prevented Connor from getting crushed. Then he looked down at the boy in his arm and repeated the special word that had brought him back to life.

"Friend!" he said, his eyes showing his friendship symbol.

Everyone watched in amazement as Cubix carried Connor to safety.

"Cubix, the unfixable robot, is fixed!" gasped Hela.

"And Connor passed his test after all!" added Chip.

With Cubix's help, the Botties Pit was soon made safe again. Then Mong reported that the stolen WeldNFix had been seen at a nearby building site. Everyone jumped onto their hover - scooters and set off.

"Cubix," puffed Connor, who had to run, "I wish we had a hover-scooter!"

"Hover-scooter," repeated Cubix, changing his shape and giving Connor the most thrilling ride of his life!

At the building site, Dr. K was about to perform an operation on the WeldNFix. Using his whirring mechanical hand, he extracted the supply of Solex from the trembling robot.

"I'm sure the operation will be a success," he snickered, cruelly, "even if you don't survive!"

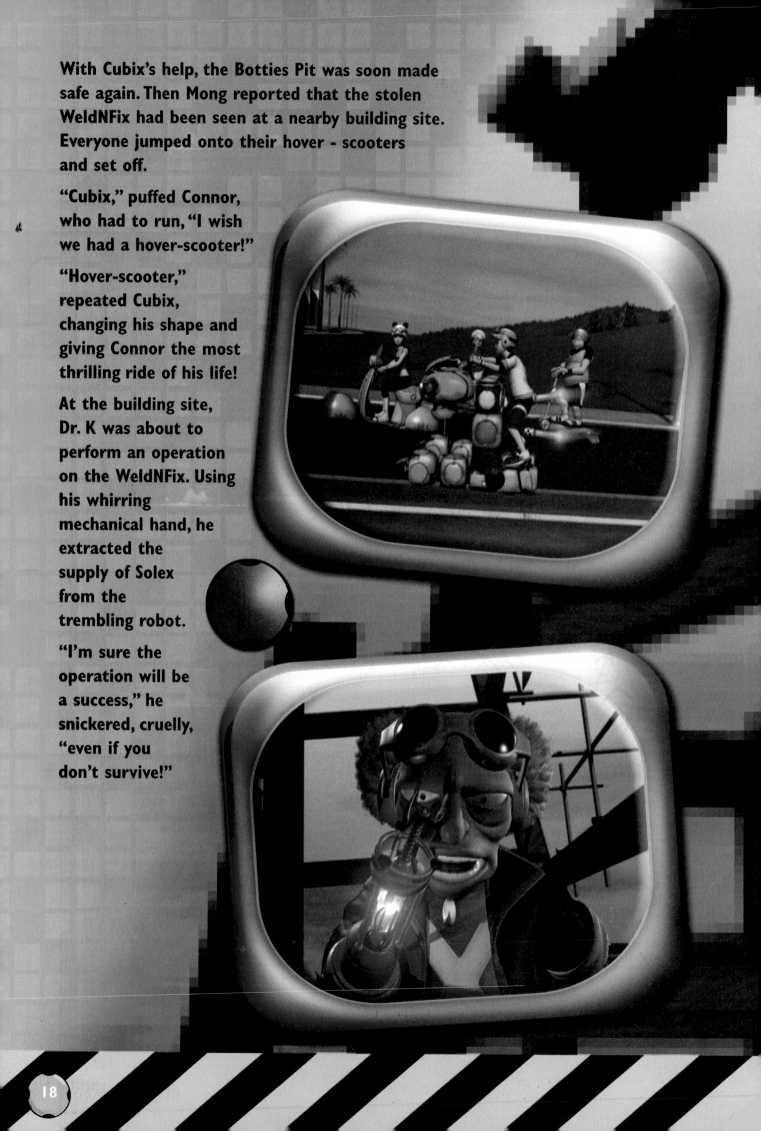

Luckily, Connor arrived before the unfortunate WeldNFix was completely destroyed.

Leaping bravely from the flying Cubix, Connor leapt on Dr. K and wrestled him to the ground. They rolled over and over in the dust.

"Why did you steal that robot?" shouted Connor.

"Why not?" retorted the wicked scientist.

Using some stink gas, Dr. K broke free of his enemy and escaped in his flying pod. But not before he had issued some deadly orders.

"Kolossal!" he called. "I'll leave you here to clean up!"

Suddenly, Connor found himself in mortal danger. Looking up, he saw the terrifying figure of Kolossal about to crush him with a huge iron girder!

Connor thought he was finished – until he heard a powerful cry that made his heart race.

"HEY! Get away!" yelled Cubix.

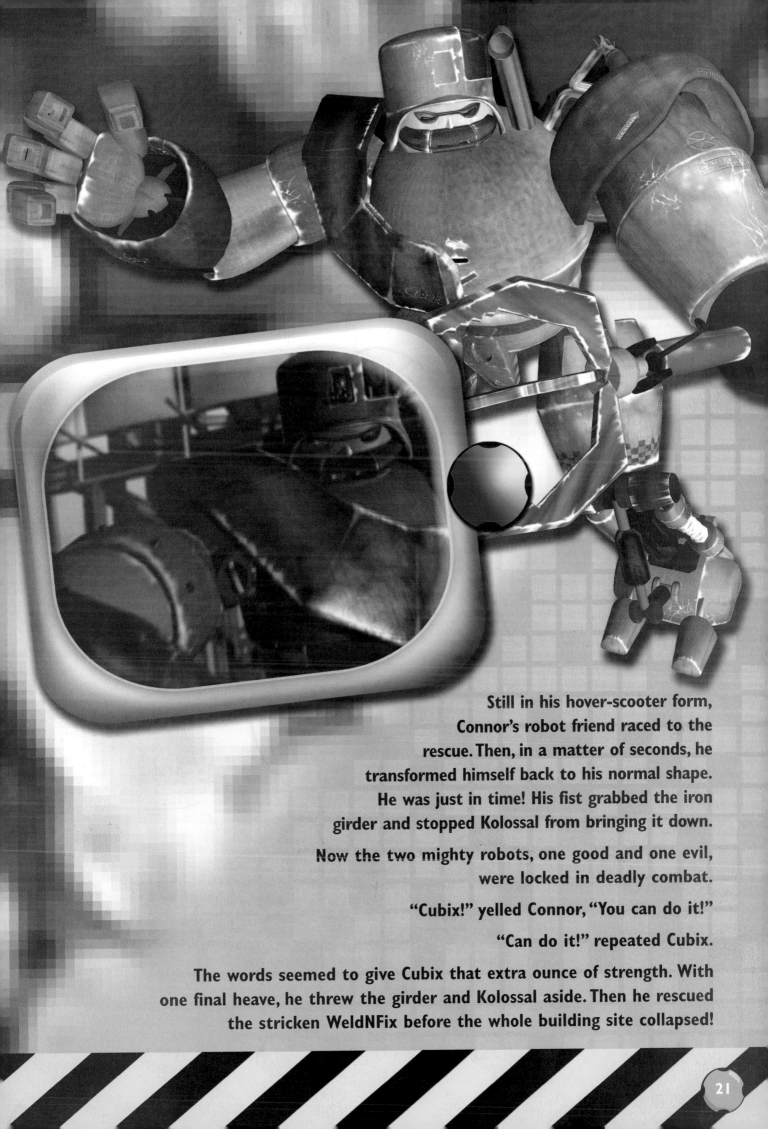

Still in his hover-scooter form, Connor's robot friend raced to the rescue. Then, in a matter of seconds, he transformed himself back to his normal shape. He was just in time! His fist grabbed the iron girder and stopped Kolossal from bringing it down.

Now the two mighty robots, one good and one evil, were locked in deadly combat.

"Cubix!" yelled Connor, "You can do it!"

"Can do it!" repeated Cubix.

The words seemed to give Cubix that extra ounce of strength. With one final heave, he threw the girder and Kolossal aside. Then he rescued the stricken WeldNFix before the whole building site collapsed!

Later that day, back at the Botties Pit, everyone cheered as Hela repaired the injured WeldNFix.

"So, Connor," asked Chip. "Are you going to join us here or what?"

"If you insist," chuckled Connor.

"If you insist," echoed Cubix.

Yet even while the friends were celebrating, Dr. K was plotting to cause more trouble in the future. Back in his lair, he showed the Alien his stolen Solex and explained how Connor had tried to stop him taking it.

"He didn't find out about the Solex, did he?" asked the Alien, angrily.

"Of course not!" snapped Dr. K.

"Good," sniggered the Alien. "Solex must remain our secret...until the time is *right!*"

Mr. FXIT™ says

COLOUR IT UP!

Mr. Fixit needs your help! He's been called in to mend a computer-colouring machine, but it needs a spare part and can't be done quickly.

Using this small insert to guide you, colour this picture of all the Bubble Town friends.

DISPOS[X]™ says RECYCLE A ROBOT!

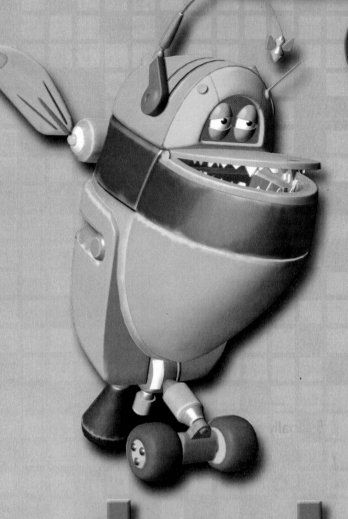

You will need:

empty tissue box large size

empty matchbox large size

PVA glue

poster paint

2 toothpaste boxes

2 toilet roll tubes

2 pipe-cleaners

Bubble Town's very own garbage-disposal pelican spends all his time picking up litter and rubbish. Disposix likes to recycle as much as he can and use it for other things – especially making models!

Follow these stage-by-stage instructions and turn some old cardboard boxes into your own special robot!

1. First of all, paint all the cardboard boxes and tubes in one colour. Leave everything to dry completely.

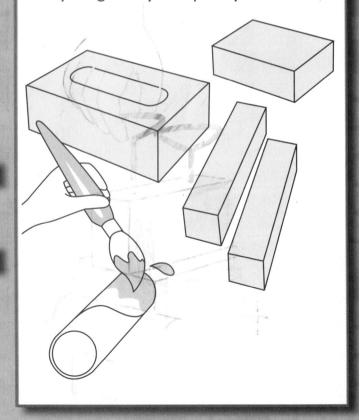

2. Stand the big tissue box upright. Glue the toothpaste boxes at the bottom to make the feet. Now glue the toilet roll tubes at the sides to make the arms.

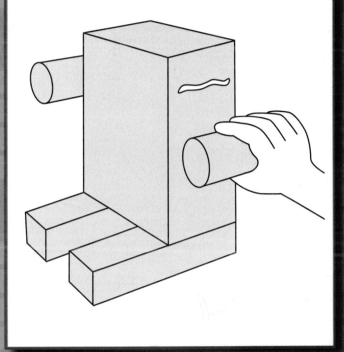

3. Glue the big matchbox across the top to make the head.

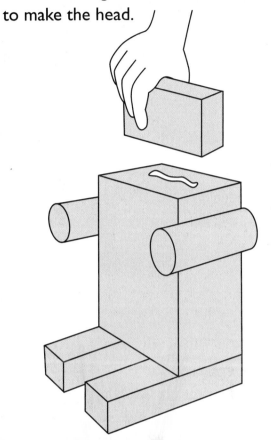

4. Bend the pipe-cleaners into any shape you want. Then push them into the top of your robot to form antennae.

5. Finally, decorate your robot.

TOUR THE TOWN!

1 Abbys house ✓

2 Conners house ✓

3 Graham @doughnut shop

4 Dr-Ks lair ✓

Hop2ix knows Bubble Town like the back of his iron hand. But how well do you know your way around Bubble Town?

To find out, Hop2ix has set these pictures of well-known Bubble Town landmarks. Identify each one and write its name underneath.

5 Robix Corp ✓

6 Botties Pit ✓

7 Garage ✗

8 Pizza shop ✓

7/8

THE UNDERGROUND OF BUBBLE TOWN

It was a normal night in Bubble Town...or, at least, it started out that way.

Connor had already gone to bed, but Abby was up late doing her homework.

"Why didn't I start this report sooner?" she sighed. "I'm gonna be up all night!"

Suddenly, without warning, there was a power failure. All the lights went out around the town and Abby's computer crashed, making her lose her work!

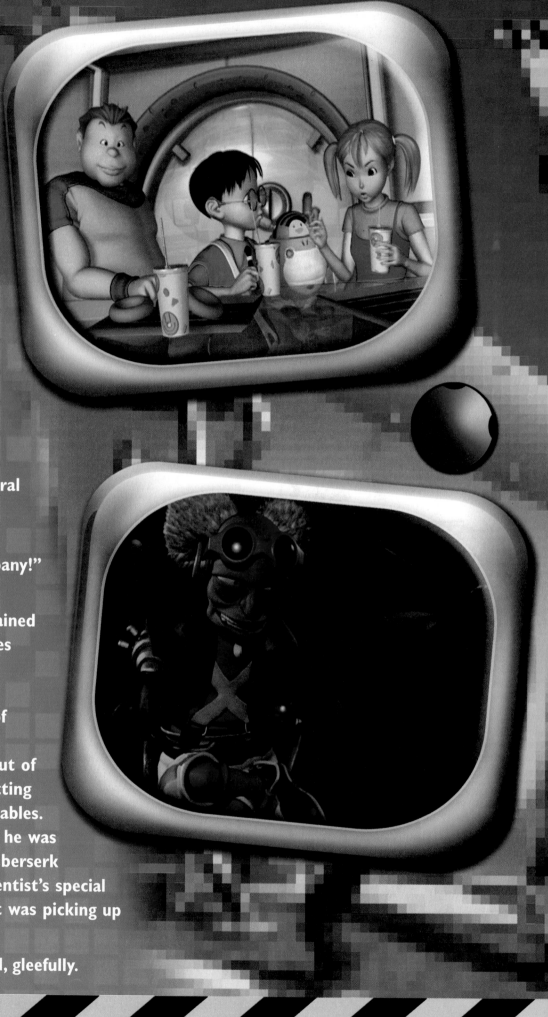

A few days later, at the Doughnut Shop run by Connor's dad, Mong and Chip watched Abby eating one doughnut after another.

"Slow down," warned Mong.

"Yeah." agreed Chip. "That's your eighth doughnut!"

But Abby was angry. There had been several more power cuts recently.

"Stupid power company!" she grumbled.

The company maintained its electricity supplies with the help of underground robots called Sewwix. One of them, nicknamed Rhymin', had gone out of control and kept cutting through the power cables. Nobody knew where he was or why he had gone berserk except Dr. K, the scientist's special detection equipment was picking up a strong signal.

"Solex!" he snickered, gleefully.

Back in the Doughnut Shop, Connor and Hela arrived with their tool-kits. They wanted to repair a Waitrix robot that was malfunctioning and driving Connor's Dad mad! By fixing the robotic waiter, Connor hoped to cure Graham of his hatred of robots.

"My dad'll come round ...you'll see." he promised.

The plan failed! Even though Hela managed to cure the problem, Graham refused to change his mind. News of the runaway Sewwix had just reached him, and he told everyone what was causing the series of power failures.

"Guess I was right about robots after all!" he muttered.

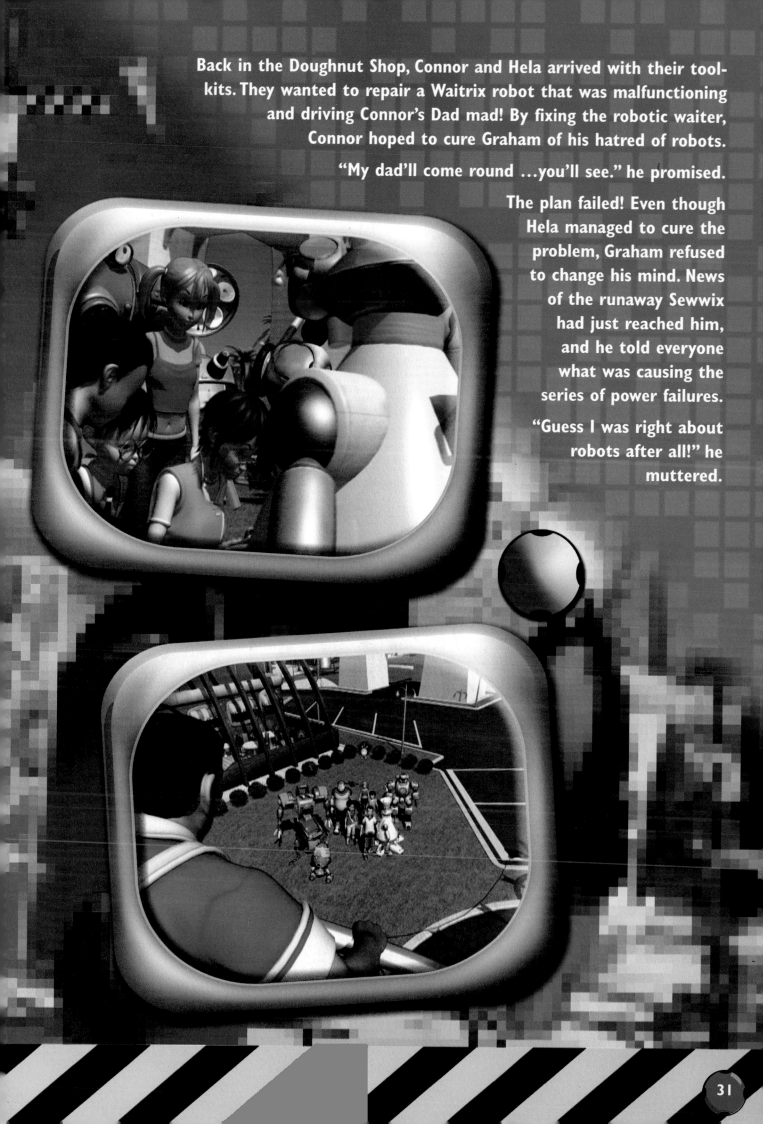

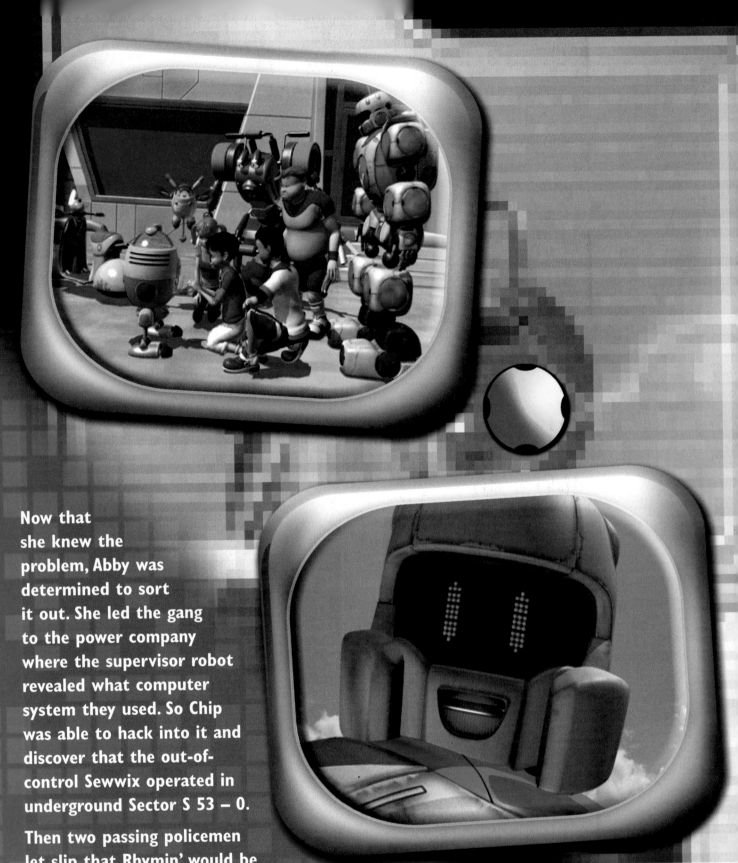

Now that
she knew the
problem, Abby was
determined to sort
it out. She led the gang
to the power company
where the supervisor robot
revealed what computer
system they used. So Chip
was able to hack into it and
discover that the out-of-
control Sewwix operated in
underground Sector S 53 – 0.

Then two passing policemen
let slip that Rhymin' would be
destroyed as soon as he was found.
That fired up Abby even more!

"We can't let 'em junk it!" she pleaded. "We have
to save the Sewwix!"

Did Cubix think it was possible? His eyes lit up in affirmative mode.
"We can!" he said.

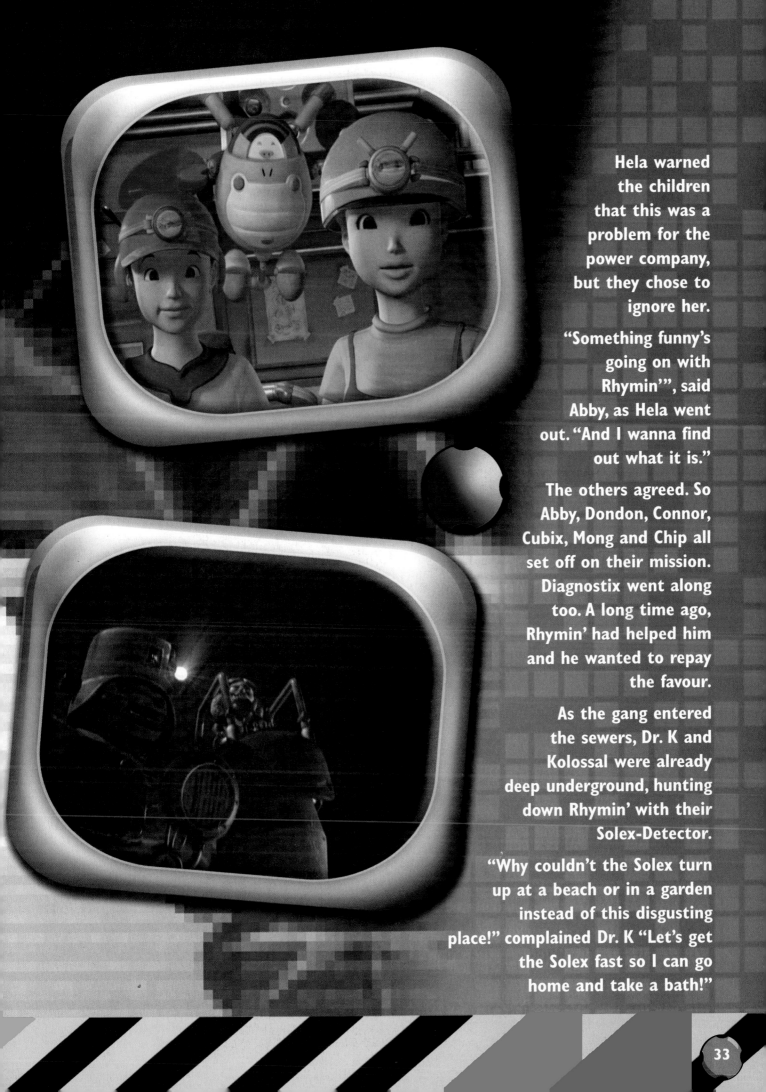

Hela warned the children that this was a problem for the power company, but they chose to ignore her.

"Something funny's going on with Rhymin'", said Abby, as Hela went out. "And I wanna find out what it is."

The others agreed. So Abby, Dondon, Connor, Cubix, Mong and Chip all set off on their mission. Diagnostix went along too. A long time ago, Rhymin' had helped him and he wanted to repay the favour.

As the gang entered the sewers, Dr. K and Kolossal were already deep underground, hunting down Rhymin' with their Solex-Detector.

"Why couldn't the Solex turn up at a beach or in a garden instead of this disgusting place!" complained Dr. K "Let's get the Solex fast so I can go home and take a bath!"

With the children hard on his heels, and Hela finding out where they were and starting to follow them, Dr. K and Kolossal closed in on Rhymin'. They found the Sewwix glaring down at them from the roof of the sewer. He was in the mood for a fight.

"Intruders in my space!" he snarled. "Makin' this place a disgrace with your ugly face. I'll erase your trace just in case!"

Of course, Rhymin' was no match for the might of Kolossal. He was soon in trouble. Which meant that the gang had to rescue him immediately – but how? Cubix provided the answer. Changing his shape, he became a transporter that carried Connor, Abby and Dondon through the dark tunnels at breakneck speed!

With help from Diagnostix, who had flown on ahead, Rhymin' just managed to prevent Kolossal from completely destroying him. Then Cubix and the children arrived, joining in the fight and managing to free the struggling Sewwix. That made Dr. K furious!

"It's those kids again!" he shrieked. "Kolossal... go get 'em!"

Suddenly, Abby and Connor found themselves looking up at the terrifying figure of Kolossal extending his deadly iron claw towards them.

Cubix came to the rescue. Transforming himself again, he went into battle mode and held his giant enemy at bay whilst the children escaped. Then, with one mighty effort, Cubix pushed Kolossal over backwards, landing on Dr. K and almost flattening him!

Now it was time to get away completely. Cubix transformed himself back into a scooter and Rhymin' was clamped to the front. Then Abby, Connor, Dondon and Diagnostix all scrambled on board and set off. They thought they were safe…until disaster stuck! The Solex inside the Sewwix made him malfunction again. Emitting an eerie white light, Rhymin' began shooting out powerful electric pulses.

"Get away," warned Connor. "He's out of control!"

Worse was to follow. One of the snaking electrical pulses disturbed the underground systems and a trapdoor appeared in the ground. Rhymin' fell down the hole, followed by Diagnostix who had been trying to calm his friend down. Abby and her friends watched helplessly as the pair disappeared into the darkness below.

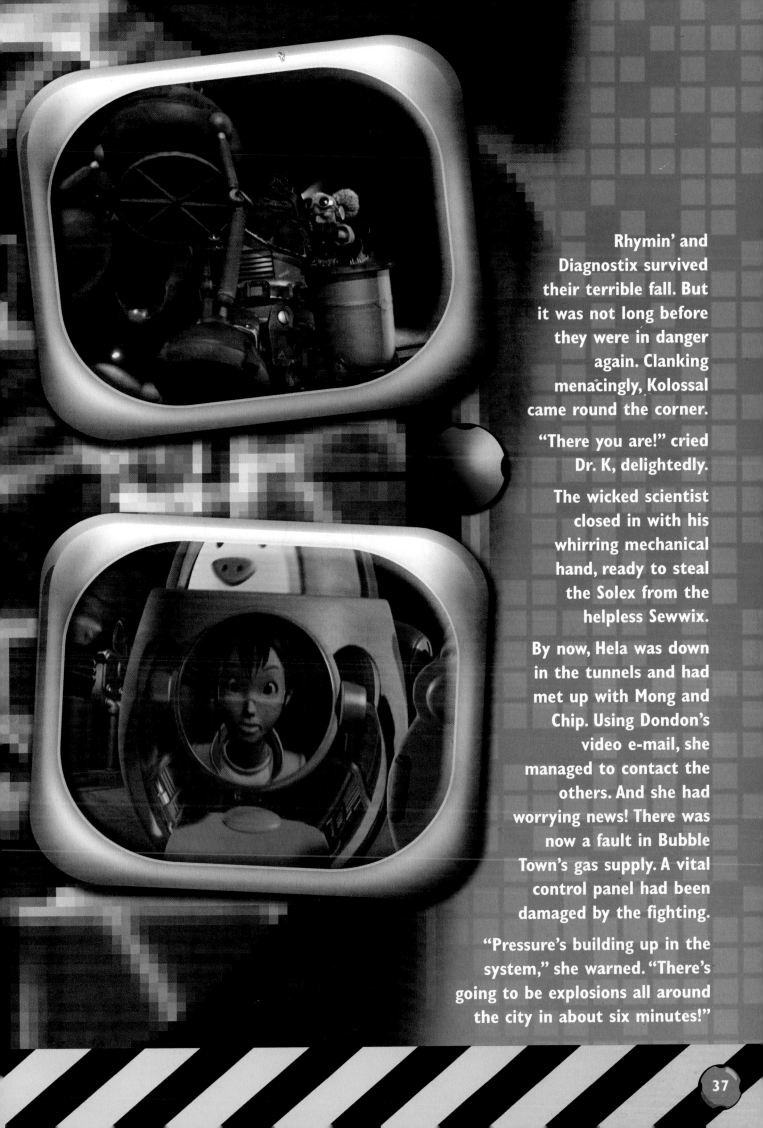

Rhymin' and Diagnostix survived their terrible fall. But it was not long before they were in danger again. Clanking menacingly, Kolossal came round the corner.

"There you are!" cried Dr. K, delightedly.

The wicked scientist closed in with his whirring mechanical hand, ready to steal the Solex from the helpless Sewwix.

By now, Hela was down in the tunnels and had met up with Mong and Chip. Using Dondon's video e-mail, she managed to contact the others. And she had worrying news! There was now a fault in Bubble Town's gas supply. A vital control panel had been damaged by the fighting.

"Pressure's building up in the system," she warned. "There's going to be explosions all around the city in about six minutes!"

Once again, Hela warned the children to get to safety — and, once again, they disobeyed her. There was no time for anyone else to save the situation.

"And don't forget we've got Cubix to protect us!" added Connor.

So Abby, Connor and Dondon sped through the tunnels again, searching for their robot friends. They arrived just as Dr. K was sucking the last of the Solex from Rhymin'. But the brave Sewwix had not been destroyed.

"You're not gonna get away this time!" shouted Connor.

Whilst Cubix grappled with Kolossal, Connor helped Rhymin' to function again and Abby struggled with the gas control panel. The computer was refusing the shut down the gas supply.

"Something's wrong!" cried Abby. "This is not working."

The newly-fixed Sewwix knew what to do.

"I know loads of codes!" chuckled Rhymin', tapping in the right one and turning off the gas just in time.

By now, the struggle between Cubix and Kolossal was nearing its climax. Together, they fell over the edge of another deep hole and plunged downwards, turning somersaults in the air. Kolossal saved himself with the use of his extending arm and Cubix flew to safety by transforming into a flying machine.

"Next time I run into you and that jigsaw puzzle you call a robot," yelled Dr. K, preparing to depart, "I'm not going to be so nice!"

One final danger remained. Even though the gas supply had been shut down, there had been a build-up of pressure in the main pipe. Suddenly, it exploded, causing a wall of billowing red fire. The only escape was to outrun it. So, with everyone hanging on for dear life, Cubix sped down the tunnels with the fire only seconds behind.

With the automatic fire-doors shutting ahead of the them, the gang managed to squeeze through just in time and soar into the clear blue sky, leaving the raging fire contained behind them.

"Connor! Abby! Are you all right?" called Hela over their radio-link.

"Couldn't be better!" laughed Connor.

Next day, at the Botties Pit, everyone rejoiced to see Rhymin' restored to full functioning and even copied his way of talking in verse.

"Outrageous!" he chuckled. "Rhymin's contagious!"

Then Hela used Ixpressive to show what Dr. K had done to the Sewwix.

"What is that stuff, Hela?" asked Abby, as they watched the wicked scientist extract the glowing substance, the most powerful energy source in the Universe.

"Solex!" whispered Hela.

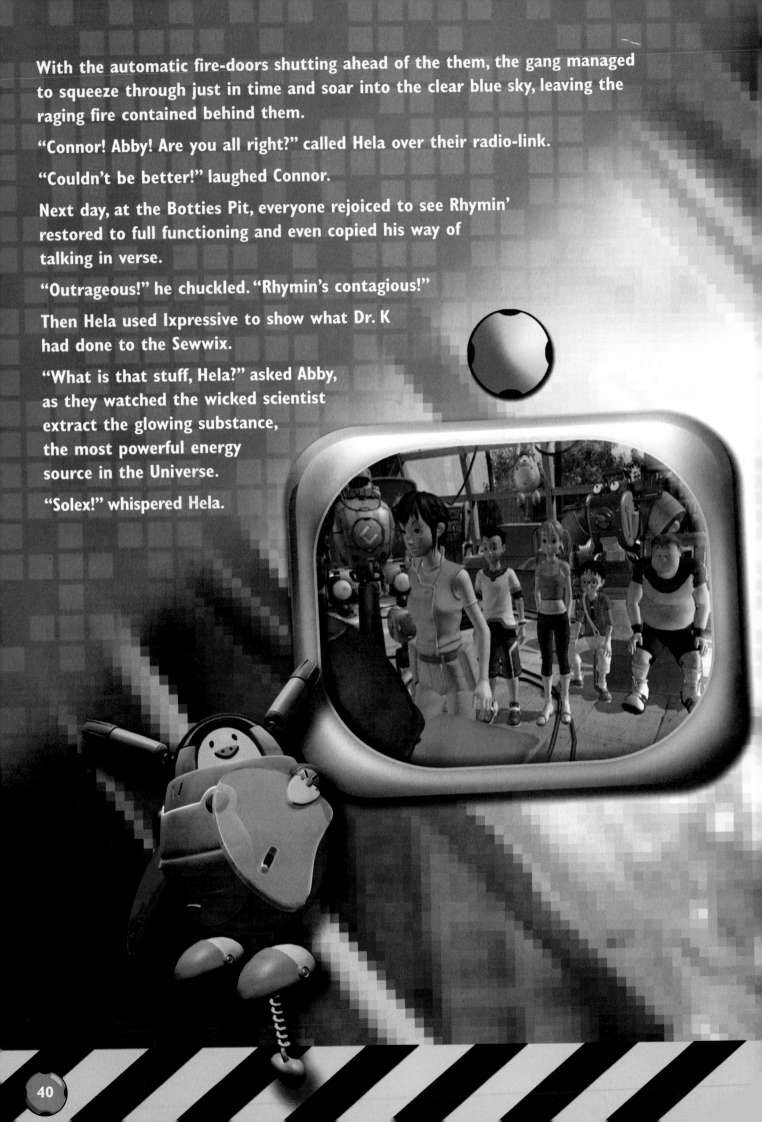

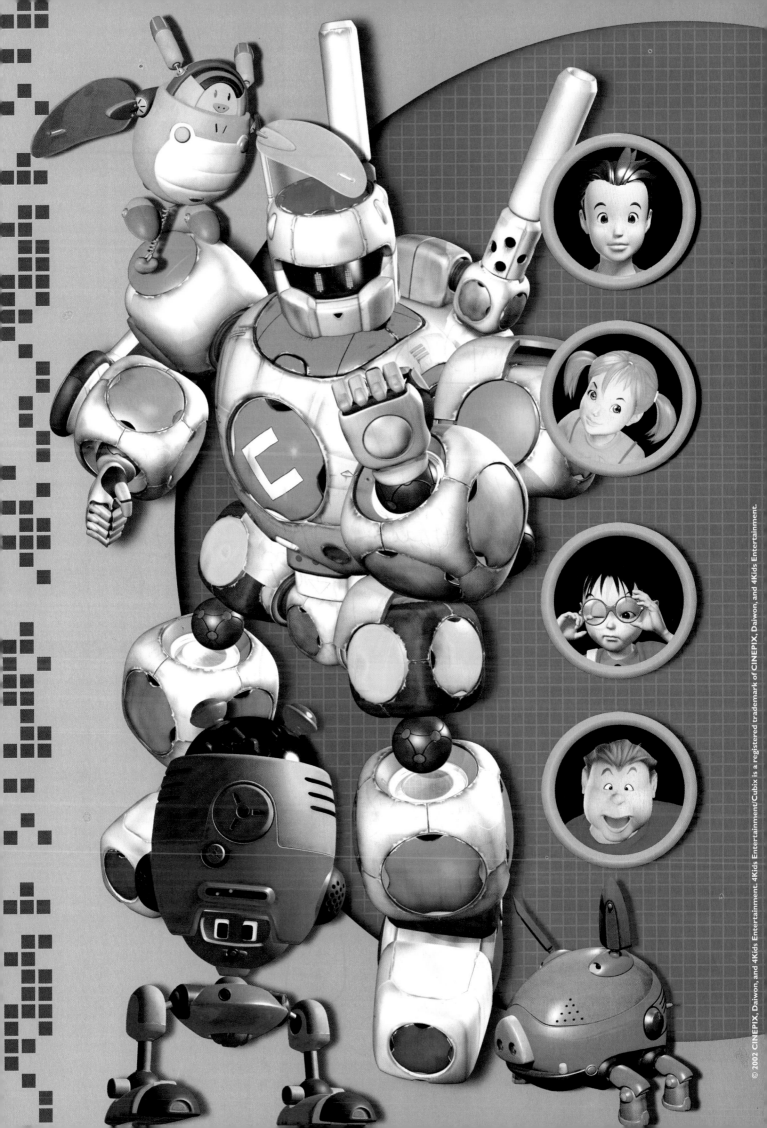

DRAW WITH ME

Some dust has blown into Chip's eye and it's affecting his photographic memory. He can only visualise one half of Quixtreme 5000. Can you help him out?

Using the grid-lines for guidance, draw in the other half of the mighty robot. Then colour your drawing in matching colours.

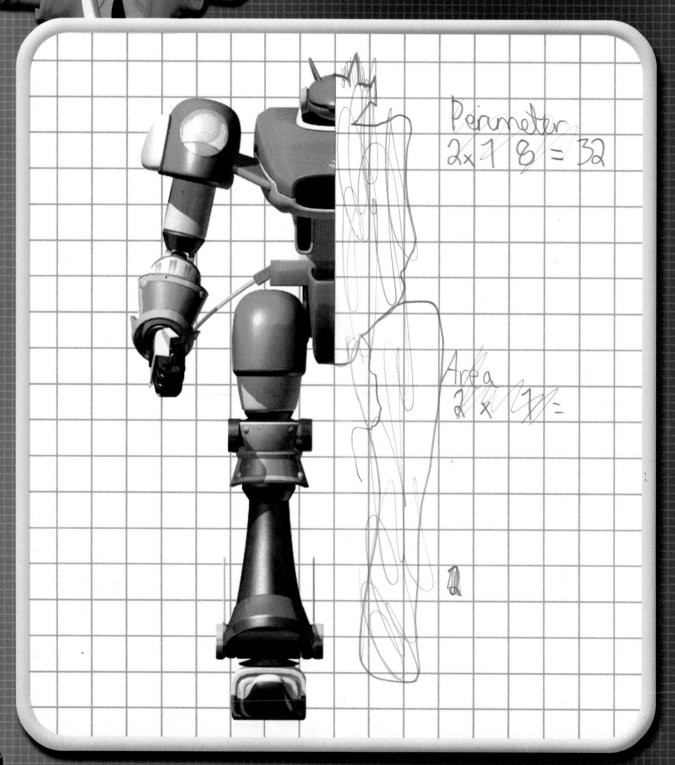

Perimeter
2x7 8 = 32

Area
2 x 7 =

MUNCH WITH ME!

YOU WILL NEED

175g dry porridge oats
100g butter or margarine
100g brown sugar (demerara)
50g desiccated coconut
3 tablespoons golden syrup
1 teaspoon baking powder
1 egg
Pinch of salt

Everyone knows how much Mong likes his food – and Flapjacks are one of his favourite snacks.

Make them for yourself by following this simple recipe.

But remember –
be safe by being sure a grown-up knows you are cooking.

WHAT YOU DO

Put the margarine, sugar and golden syrup into a saucepan. Warm very gently until everything has melted.

Take off the stove and stir in the porridge oats and coconut.

Break the egg into a cup, beat it up and stir into the mixture.

Add the salt and baking powder.

Rub the margarine wrapper round a baking tin to grease it and prevent sticking.

Pour the mixture into the baking tin and press it down all round.

Put in the oven and bake for about 25 minutes on Gas Mark 4 / 180 C

Remove from oven and leave to cool for 5 minutes.

Cut into 12 or 16 squares and remove from tin.

enjoy!

KNOW YOUR EPU!

Nobody knows the robots of Bubble Town better than Hela. Fixing them every day in her Botties Pit, Hela has learned to keep a close eye on each robot's EPU (Emotional Processing Unit) to see how it is feeling.

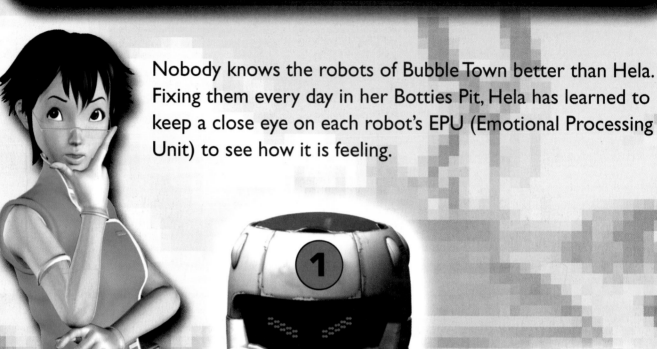

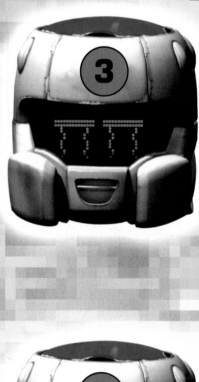

How well can you read Cubix's emotions? To test you, Hela has set these ten pictures and wants you to write the feeling that each one shows in the space underneath.

1. Angry
2. bright Idea
3. I agree
4. confused
5. can't stand
6. Get off
7. LOVE
8. computeretix
9. Sorry
10. Ferocious

HELP ME FIND DONDON!

Normally, Dondon keeps in touch with Abby via his in-built camera. But a force-field from a robot scrapyard has made this equipment malfunction. So Dondon is helpless!

Help Abby to rescue her beloved robot by finding the ONE PATH through the metal pipe maze.

FIXED COMPETITION

The assembly hall
in Bubble Town was
packed to the rafters.
Everyone wanted to see the
Bubble Town Talent Show in which
robots competed to show off their amazing
skills. Cubix got through the qualifying rounds by
turning himself into a gigantic pile of cubes.

"Let's wish all our contestants good luck," said the robot
announcer, "as they prepare for the final round."

Cubix, Maximix and Cerebrix were all in the final. So, back at the Botties Pit, the robots practiced their routines in front of Hela. Cubix showed how his head could fly round on its own. And Cerebrix did a little song and dance – until he fell over! But Mong refused to show what Maximix could do.

"He's got a new secret talent that'll blow the judges away!" he chuckled.

Then Abby arrived with Dondon. They had exciting news!

Abby had been doing a history project for school. She had found a photo of Professor Nemo, the famous founder of RobixCorp. It was taken just before the accident that had blown his lab apart and it showed a line of special robots.

"All those robots had Solex!" muttered Chip.

What excited Abby was that one of the robots was still around today. It was called a Mozzarelix.

"Pizza Boy!" everyone cried.

Solex was the most powerful energy source in the Universe. The evil scientist, Dr. K, wanted to get his hands on as much of it as possible — and the Botties were determined to stop him. So they set out in search of Pizza Boy in the hope of finding the Solex inside him. Unfortunately, there were several Mozzarelix robots around the town, and the right one could not be found.

Later, outside the Town Hall, Charles arrived with his robot, The Quixtreme 5000. Charles was the Mayor's son, rich and spoiled, and he was quick to boast that Quixtreme 5000, would win the contest.

"A definite first place," he bragged. "No two ways about it."

The Quixtreme 5000, a sleek, cat-shaped robot, was bursting with uncontrolled energy!

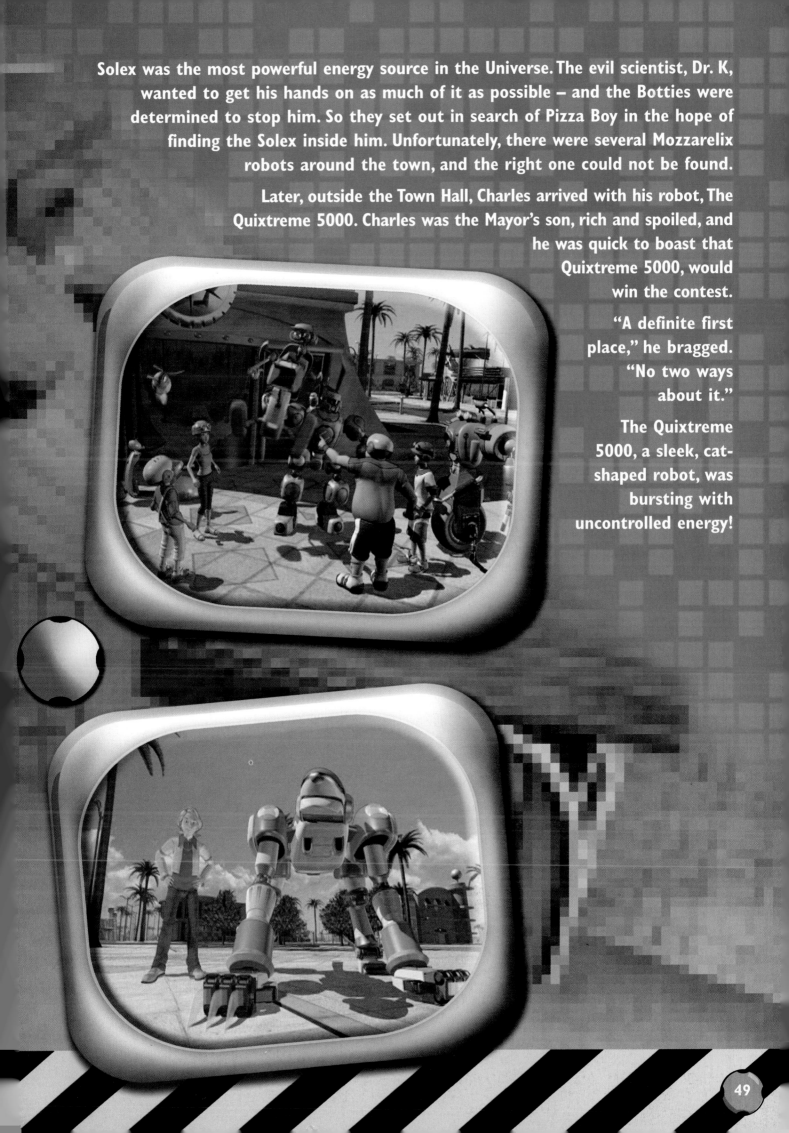

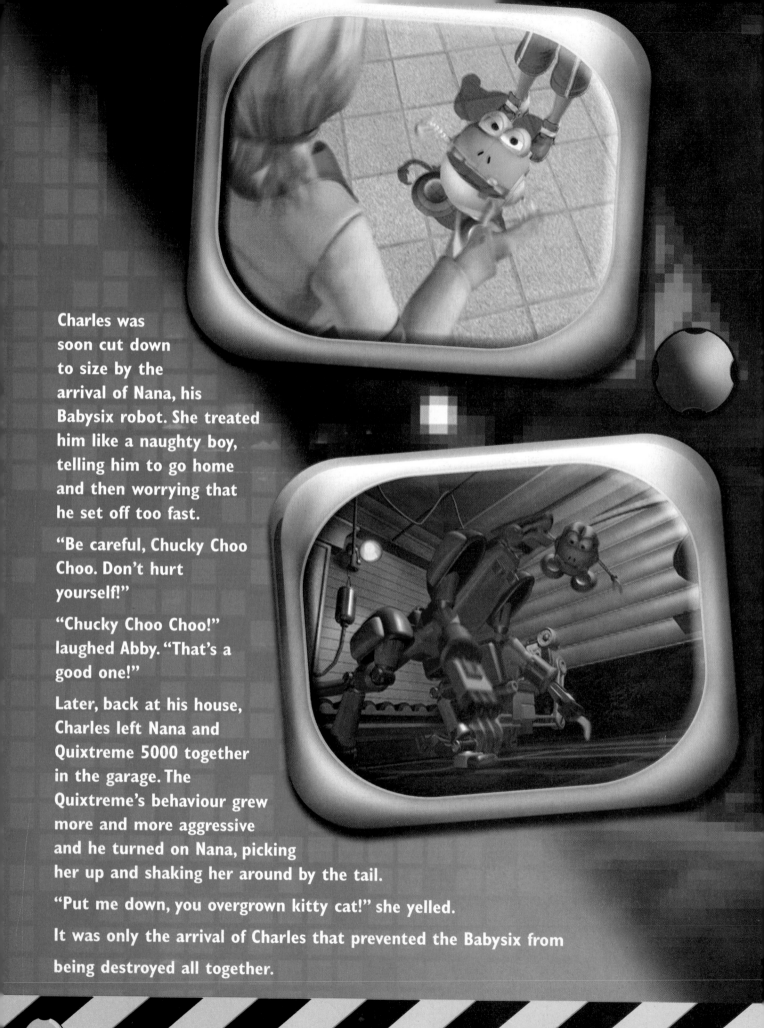

Charles was soon cut down to size by the arrival of Nana, his Babysix robot. She treated him like a naughty boy, telling him to go home and then worrying that he set off too fast.

"Be careful, Chucky Choo Choo. Don't hurt yourself!"

"Chucky Choo Choo!" laughed Abby. "That's a good one!"

Later, back at his house, Charles left Nana and Quixtreme 5000 together in the garage. The Quixtreme's behaviour grew more and more aggressive and he turned on Nana, picking her up and shaking her around by the tail.

"Put me down, you overgrown kitty cat!" she yelled.

It was only the arrival of Charles that prevented the Babysix from being destroyed all together.

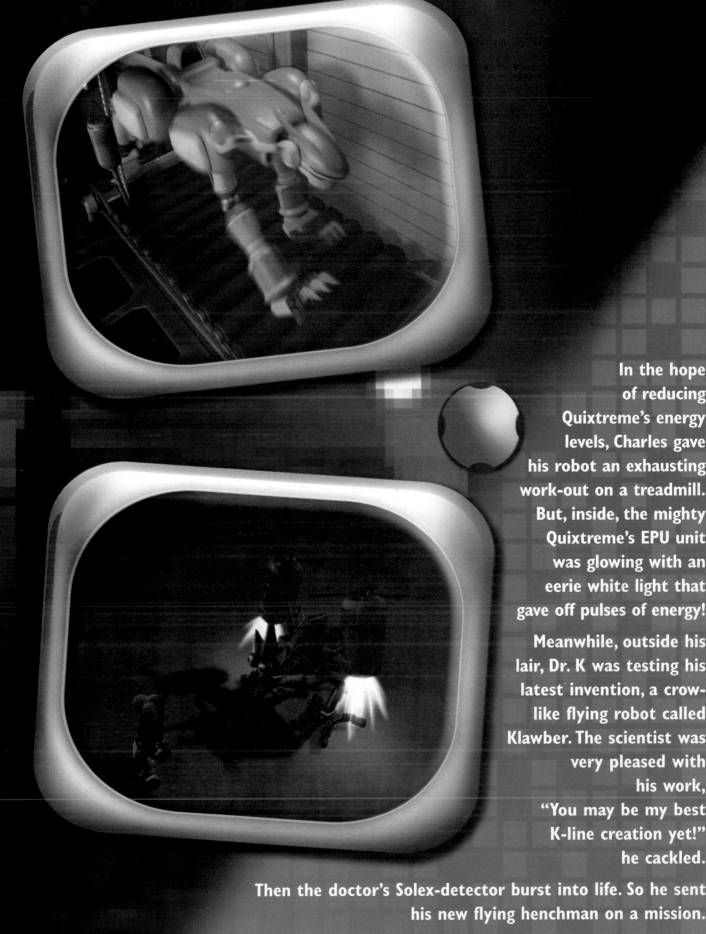

In the hope of reducing Quixtreme's energy levels, Charles gave his robot an exhausting work-out on a treadmill. But, inside, the mighty Quixtreme's EPU unit was glowing with an eerie white light that gave off pulses of energy!

Meanwhile, outside his lair, Dr. K was testing his latest invention, a crow-like flying robot called Klawber. The scientist was very pleased with his work, "You may be my best K-line creation yet!" he cackled.

Then the doctor's Solex-detector burst into life. So he sent his new flying henchman on a mission.

"There's Solex out here!" he cries. "Go and find it, Klawber!"

By now, it was time for the Final of the Talent Contest. Charles and Quixtreme 5000 were already inside when the Botties arrived. They spoke to Nana who revealed that Quixtreme 5000 had been in Professor Nemo's lab when it exploded. The Quixtreme was only slightly damaged and replaced a destroyed Mozzarelix as Charles's birthday gift. That explained why the gang could not find the missing Pizza Boy – and why Charles's companion was out of control.

"Quixtreme 5000 has Solex!" gasped Abby.

The effect of this all-powerful substance was soon plain to see. Inside the hall, Quixtreme 5000 went completely berserk! Growling like a wounded tiger, the powerful robot picked up one of the judges and carried him outside.

"This is outrageous!" protested the judge. "Let me down!"

Quixtreme's response was to throw the yelling official into a pond!

Then Quixtreme 5000 turned on his master and the gang! The youngsters stood wide-eyed with fear as the giant cat-shaped robot pounded towards them, snarling savagely. But Cubix was there to protect them. Stepping forwards, he barred the way and then threw Quixtreme 5000 backwards.

"Way to go, Cubix!" cheered Connor.

The setback made the Quixtreme even angrier. He returned to the fight and knocked Cubix over with one mighty blow. Now Connor's robot was completely at his mercy!

Help arrived from a most unexpected and unwelcome source! Swooping down from the sky, Klawber snatched the Quixtreme 5000 in his iron talons. Dr. K's flying robot wanted the Solex that was making Quixtreme 5000 malfunction so badly. Charles could not bear to see his robot taken, so he clung on to Klawber.

"Oh, my Chucky!" gasped a horrified Nana, as Charles was carried high into the air.

There was only one way to save Charles and the Quixtreme 5000.

"All right, Cubix. Hit it!" ordered Connor.

"Hit it!" repeated Cubix.

Transforming into a high-speed flying machine, Cubix sped after their kidnapped friends with Connor sitting fearlessly at the controls.

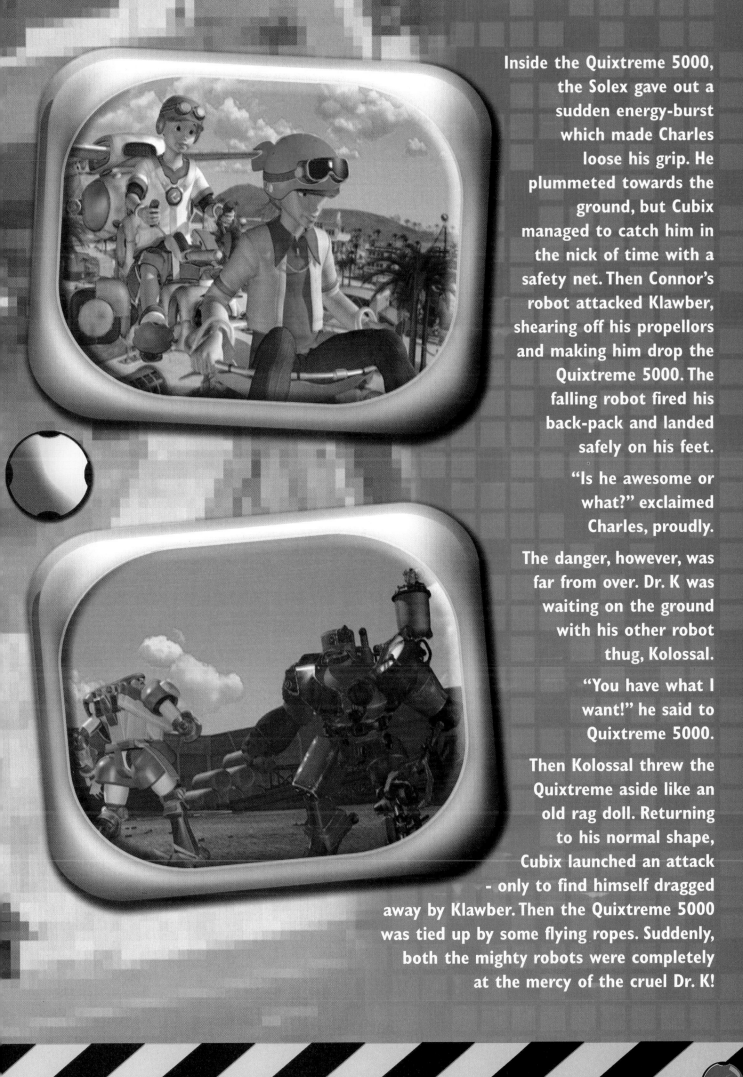

Inside the Quixtreme 5000, the Solex gave out a sudden energy-burst which made Charles loose his grip. He plummeted towards the ground, but Cubix managed to catch him in the nick of time with a safety net. Then Connor's robot attacked Klawber, shearing off his propellors and making him drop the Quixtreme 5000. The falling robot fired his back-pack and landed safely on his feet.

"Is he awesome or what?" exclaimed Charles, proudly.

The danger, however, was far from over. Dr. K was waiting on the ground with his other robot thug, Kolossal.

"You have what I want!" he said to Quixtreme 5000.

Then Kolossal threw the Quixtreme aside like an old rag doll. Returning to his normal shape, Cubix launched an attack - only to find himself dragged away by Klawber. Then the Quixtreme 5000 was tied up by some flying ropes. Suddenly, both the mighty robots were completely at the mercy of the cruel Dr. K!

All this time, Hela and the others had been looking on helplessly. Now Mong decided to act. He dispatched Maximix, his robot, to perform the secret skill he had been saving up for the Talent Show.

"He's the pumpinator!" yelled Mong. "He rocks!"

His fists inflated like giant punchbags, Maximix dealt Kolossal a huge blow that sent the monster reeling. But, immediately afterwards, Maximix ran out of power!

"Toss that flat tyre on the garbage heap!" ordered Dr. K.

With everyone now defeated, Charles rushed into the fight himself.

"I'm the Mayor's son and nobody pushes me like that!" he shouted.

"Then we'd better come up with a new way to push you around!" retorted Dr. K. Kolossal stepped forward to crush Charles. So Nana leapt into the fray, desperate to protect her charge. She clung on to Kolossal's arm, preventing him from using it.

"Throw her all the way to the Town Hall!" commanded Dr. K.

For a moment, it seemed that all was lost. Then Cubix, who was still pinned to the ground, managed to throw Klawber off and then transform himself into a flying saucer.

Spinning through the air, he hit Kolossal in the chest and sent the monster flying! But Klawber was not finished. With an enraged squawk, he unleashed two deadly missiles that followed Cubix wherever he turned.

Now it was Connor's turn to use the special skills practiced for the Talent Show.

"Cubix!" he called. "Heads up!"

"Heads up!" echoed Cubix, detaching his head from his body and making it fly alone. Then the amazing robot performed a clever manoeuvre. He flew right past Klawber so that the following missiles smashed into their owner, destroying him!

"That's using your head, Cubix!" chuckled Connor.

The following day, Charles called at the Botties Pit to collect the Quixtreme 5000. Hela had removed the Solex and repaired the damaged robot.

"Without Solex," laughed Abby, "Quixtreme's like a pussy cat!"

Charles was grateful for all the help he had been given. So he swallowed his pride and made friends.

"I guess you're all right, Connor," he murmured, shaking hands. "And…uh…Cubix is too!"

Then Nana arrived. The previous day, Kolossal's mighty throw had landed her in the town hall. Her sudden arrival, followed by a comical trip as she ran across the stage, amused the judges so much that they awarded her act first prize!

"I've been asked to join a travelling dance company!" she announced, excitedly.

Then she tried her new dance routine. The way she kept tripping over reduced everyone to fits of helpless laughter!

© 2002 CINEPIX, Daiwon, and 4Kids Entertainment. 4Kids Entertainment/Cubix is a registered trademark of CINEPIX, Daiwon, and 4Kids Entertainment.

BUILD-A-BOT!

Do you think you've got what it takes to be an Official Robot Designer for RobixCorp™? Well, over 30,000 Cubix fans did and they entered Cartoon Network's Build-a-Bot contest. The challenge was to design a new Cubix robot and the winner's robot gets to appear in a future episode of Cubix!

After hours and hours of opening envelopes and looking at all of the entries, a shortlist was sent to New York for the creators of Cubix to choose the overall winner. The judges were not just looking for a great design, but also had to find a robot that would fit into the new storylines for Cubix. The lucky winner was 10-year old Daniel Driver from Leeds, who designed Correctix, a clever lab robot, who can help you do your sums and identify if you've got a wrong answer and tell you what to do next – just like a live calculator!

Don't forget to look out for Daniel's robot, Correctix, early next year!

Thomas Moreton, age 9.

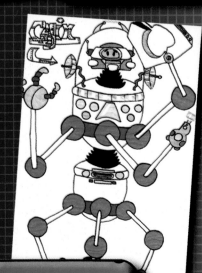

Ben Scullin, age 14.

Leah Bewes, age 5.

CORRECTIX

Correctix is extremely smart. He can correct you whenever you make the wrong decision or answer. Correctix will be excellent for a Lab robot.

Specs for accurate inspections

Lights up when right

Lights up when wrong

Tells you which function to use for a number problem

Alarm for emergency correction

WINNER!

Daniel Driver, age 10.

Why not have a go at designing your own RobixCorp™ Robot too!

Readarton

Readarton will be fun to have around because he can read books to you, private note (he could be used to read your reader at school.) You slip the book in a slot here, and then he will read the book to you. So Readarton will be fun to have as your robot.

lights for alarm for correction for reading

alarm for correct but hard word

Slip book in and he reads to you